Disney
✦ PRINCESS
Belle

Published by Ladybird Books Ltd.,
80 Strand, London WC2R 0RL
A Penguin Company
Penguin Books Australia Ltd., Camberwell, Victoria, Australia
Penguin Books (NZ) Ltd., Private Bag 102902, NSMC, Auckland, New Zealand

Copyright © 2003 Disney Enterprises, Inc.
LADYBIRD and the device of a ladybird are trademarks of Ladybird Books, Ltd.
All rights reserved. No part of this publication may be reproduced, stored in a retrieval
system, or transmitted in any form or by any means, electronic, mechanical, photocopying,
recording or otherwise, without the prior consent of the copyright owner.

2 4 6 8 10 9 7 5 3 1

Printed in China

Belle
A Feast in the Forest

Ladybird

*B*elle rushed into the palace kitchen. "Today is the Beast's birthday!" she told her friends. "Will there be a party?"

"Oh, no," said Mrs Potts. "The Beast has always been so lonely that he's never celebrated his birthday."

"How sad!" said Belle. "Why don't we plan a special birthday feast for him?"

They prepared lots of tasty things to eat which Belle packed safely into a basket.

When the delicious treats were all packed and ready, Belle wrote a note asking the Beast to meet her in the gardens at lunchtime.

"Deliver this as soon as I've gone," she told Lumiere, and skipped off towards the palace gardens.

*B*elle made her way to a secret glade, and set everything out for the feast.

It looks nice, she thought. But it could look even more special. The Beast loves wild flowers, so I'll pick some for him.

Belle didn't see the hungry rabbits and squirrels who scurried into the clearing as soon as her back was turned. Luckily, some little birds fluttering around saw everything.

When Belle came back with the flowers, the rabbits and squirrels ran into the forest. All the food was gone!

"The picnic is ruined!" she wept.

Belle's sobs were interrupted by a bird singing in the branches above. She realised that she had laid out the picnic beneath a cherry tree, laden with fruit!

"Cherries are delicious!" Belle said. "Maybe we can have a feast after all."

*B*ut even with the cherries she picked, and some nuts the birds had gathered, there wasn't enough for a proper feast.

"Oh no, it's almost time for the Beast to arrive," Belle said, sounding worried.

Suddenly a voice rang out. "Help is at hand, Mademoiselle!" It was Lumiere – with Cogsworth, Mrs Potts and Chip right behind him!

*B*est of all, Mrs Potts had a wonderful surprise. Balanced on her spout was the most beautiful birthday cake Belle had ever seen!

"After you left, we decided we wanted to give the Beast something special, too," explained Cogsworth. "So we asked the stove to bake him this birthday cake."

"The cake is magnificent!" exclaimed Belle. "The Beast will love it! Thank you all so much!"

"Let's get ready," said Cogsworth. "The Beast will be here any minute!"

Belle set out the cake, with the flowers Belle had picked, the cherries and the nuts.

Everything was ready.

The Beast arrived at just that moment. He was amazed to see the picnic and the beautiful cake. The surprise made him so happy that he danced Belle all around the garden while the birds sang above.

Soon everyone was dancing, laughing and having a wonderful time.

"This is the best birthday I've ever had," laughed the Beast. "And it's all thanks to my very best friends!"